ROS ASQUITH has been a *Guardian* cartoonist for 20 years,
and has written and illustrated over 60 books for young people,
including the international bestsellers, *The Great Big Book of Families*
and *The Great Big Book of Feelings* with Mary Hoffman,
Max the Champion with Sean Stockdale and Alexandra Strick,
and the *Teenage Worrier* series.

She graduated from Camberwell School of Art,
working as a photographer, designer and teacher before becoming
a theatre critic for *Time Out* and the *Observer*, and diary writer
for the TV Times. Her other titles, for Barn Owl Books,
are *The Roman Beanfeast* and *The Skiver's Guide*.
Ros has two sons and lives in north London.

* Dressing-up Fairy

* Ice-cream Fairy

* Fairy-cake Fairy

* Scary Fairy

* Fruit Fairy

* Scribble Fairy

* Cooking Fairy

* Housework Fairy

* The It's Not Fairy

* Tea Fairy

For Lenny and Lola
who never, never hardly ever say 'It's Not Fair'.
And for Judith Escreet for her lovely design.

JANETTA OTTER-BARRY BOOKS

IT'S NOT Fairy

Ros Asquith

Can you find me every time you turn a page? Look very carefully, sometimes I'm hiding.

F

FRANCES LINCOLN
CHILDREN'S BOOKS

Billy had an ice-cream,
Mary had a pear.

Mary was a Zebra,
Billy was a Bear.
Mary won a prize.

"Now listen here, Billy,
and listen here, Mary.

You don't want to mess with the
It's Not Fairy!

The *It's Not Fairy* flaps round all night,
sorting out what's wrong or right.
But there's so many kids saying it's not fair,
she's ranting and raving and tearing her hair.
She's shouting, *'The very next kids I meet,
I'm pretty sure I'm going to eat!'"*

"Huh!" said Billy. "Hah!" said Mary.

"Well, she believes in YOU,
so don't blame us
if she roasts you and toasts you
for making a fuss.

She gnaws knobbly knees
(with ketchup and peas).
She scoffs boiled head
(with honey, on bread).
She guzzles kids' legs
(with bacon and eggs).

Want to know her
favourite treat?
Minced-eyes pies
and fresh fried FEET."

PUSS PIE

Dad washed the dishes.

"Does anybody care?
No one lifts a finger.
IT'S NOT FAIR!"

"Aha!" said Billy.   "Oho!" said Mary.

"You might get a visit from the *It's Not Fairy!*"

Dad roared, Mum bellowed:
"DON'T YOU DARE!
It's up to us to say what's FAIR!"

LEPRECHAUN LATEST

IT'S NOT FAIRY EATS VILLAGE

Goblin Gazette

GRIZZLING GIRLS GRILLED

DWARVES DAILY.

RECIPES: BOY BURGER

FAIRY FACTS

MORE MOANING IN MONACO

Pixie Paper

COMPLAINING CHAOS IN CANADA

Gremlin Guardian

FAIRY FURY

"Oh no, it's not!"
said a furious voice.
"Fairness is not just a matter of choice.
If you want to live fairly
you'll have to agree
that life isn't just about

Me,

Me,

Me!"

ELFIN EXTRA

WHINING IN WASHINGTON

The *It's Not Fairy* flew into a rage.
She picked up this book and
she chewed the next page...

"I'll eat your toys,

your TV too,

I'll eat your parents,

and then I'll eat YOU!

I'm sick of your squawking.
Now give me a break.
Or I'll bake you all
in a Fairy cake!"

"Oh, don't hurt Mum! Don't eat Dad!
We promise you they're not all bad.
We'll do our best to put things right."

It's Not Fairy
MENU

TV dinner
Sofa sorbet
Carpet casserole
Boiled Billy (with beans)
Minced Mary (with mash)
Fried Father (with PArmesan)
Marinaded Mother (with MAngo)

"Humph!" said the Fairy.
"I'll be back tonight!"

Here's where
the It's Not Fairy
chewed ↓

"What's really unfair?"
said Billy to Mary.
"Let's make a list for the
It's Not Fairy."

List for The IT's NOT FAIRY
by Mary
BY BILLY
by Billy AND Mary

some kids CAN **JUMP** higher, **RUN** FASTER, **Wiggle** their **EARS**, watch more T.V. Have more **TOYS**, eat **SWEETS** every **DAY**, read **WHOLE BOOKS**, walk **TIGHTROPES** do CARTWHEELS and **JUGGLE** BANANAS (But **MOST KIDS** can't)

LIFE isn't always **FAIR**

The Fairy flew in and threw off her shoes,
and fell on the sofa.
"I must have a snooze.
Been a terrible day of whining and groaning
and grousing and grouching
and whingeing and moaning."

She glanced at the list. "Humph. Looks OK.
I suppose I should say that you've made my day.
But I'm ranting and raving and near despair,
cos there's no one to eat!

IT'S NOT FAIR!"

"You're saying it now!" said Billy and Mary.
"You're not allowed! You're the *It's Not Fairy*."

"Whoops," said the Fairy, turning quite red.

"I'm allowed to complain when I've got a sore head."

Mum snorted, Dad shouted, "Let's all of us moan,
and grouse and complain and grizzle and groan."

So they griped and complained till,
collapsing with laughter,
they all lived FAIRLY ever after.

(Well . . . almost . . .)

When you've made your list for the *It's Not Fairy*
you might like to bake some IT'S NOT FAIRY CAKES.
Remember to complain all the time while you're making them.
Oh, and DO spill the milk and lots of flour, so that
the grown-ups can have a good moan too. It's only fair.

It's Not Fairy Cakes Recipe

One bad-tempered Fairy. Leave her out if she promises
to leave you in peace. Otherwise mince her finely
with a Bad Fairy mincer. (Don't use an Elf mincer, the holes
are too big. A Gnome mincer will give a very coarse texture.
If you have a Fairy Godmother, don't use her mincer.
You'll turn into a pumpkin.)

* 175 g (1½ cups) self-raising flour
* 1 level tsp baking powder
* 175 g (1 cup) caster sugar
* 175 g (1½ sticks) butter, softened
* 1 tsp vanilla extract
* 3 eggs, lightly beaten
* 250 g (2 cups) royal icing sugar
* 1 tbsp water
* Fairy Dust (it's usually called 'Edible Glitter')

How to bake It's Not Fairy Cakes

✷ Preheat the oven to 180c (355F, Gas mark 4).

✷ Line a 12-hole muffin tray with paper muffin cases.

✷ Sift the flour, baking powder and a pinch of salt into a large bowl.

✷ Add minced fairy if needed. In a separate bowl, whisk the sugar, butter and vanilla extract with an electric whisk until light and fluffy.

✷ Slowly whisk in the eggs, then with a large spoon, gradually add the flour.

✷ Fill each paper case with a large tablespoon of mixture.

✷ Persuade a grown-up to place the tray in the preheated oven and bake for 12 to 15 minutes or until golden on top.

✷ Persuade a grown-up to remove the It's Not Fairy Cakes from the tray and leave to cool on a wire rack.

✷ To make the icing, put the icing sugar in a bowl and drop in very small amounts of water, mixing until the icing is thick but glossy. Spoon the icing onto the cakes. Sprinkle on the Fairy Dust (you can use drops of food colour to make the icing different colours).

Remember to leave one cake over for the *It's Not Fairy.*

He had TWO

He broke the egg

I did NOT

Did!

It's Not FAIR

Didn't!

IT'S NOT FAIR

* Dressing-up Fairy

* Ice-cream Fairy

* Fairy-cake Fairy

* Scary Fairy

* Fruit Fairy

* Scribble Fairy

* Cooking Fairy

* Housework Fairy

* Tea Fairy

* The It's Not Fairy

MORE PICTURE BOOKS ILLUSTRATED BY ROS ASQUITH
FROM FRANCES LINCOLN CHILDREN'S BOOKS

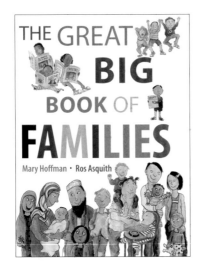

THE GREAT BIG BOOK OF FAMILIES
Written by Mary Hoffman

"A celebration of families and the very many different things they do and the very many different ways they do them. Thoughtfully explained and joyfully illustrated."
– *Julia Eccleshare, LoveReading*

THE GREAT BIG BOOK OF FEELINGS
Written by Mary Hoffman

How do you feel today? Happy? Sad? Jealous? Excited? Silly? Or a mixture of all these and more…? Explore lots of different feelings with the children in this book, see if you can find feelings that match your own, or that help you understand how other people are feeling… And look out for Tiger the cat on every page. He has feelings too!

MAX THE CHAMPION
Written by Sean Stockdale and Alexandra Strick

Max is mad about sport – and all through his school day he imagines himself competing in world-class sporting championships – from football and cycling to diving, bobsleigh and discus. But maybe Max and his friends can win a real sporting trophy too. This inspirational and inclusive picture book is perfect for ALL children who love sport.

Frances Lincoln titles are available from all good bookshops.
You can also buy books and find out more about your favourite titles,
authors and illustrators on our website: www.franceslincoln.com